# FOR THE LIFE OF ME

KELLIE JACKSON

Copyright © 2020 by Kellie Jackson

All rights reserved. No part of this publication may be reproduced, distributed, or transmitted in any form or by any means, including photocopying, recording, or other electronic or mechanical methods, without the prior written permission of the publisher, except in the case of brief quotations embodied in critical reviews and certain other noncommercial uses permitted by copyright law.

Printed in the United States of America

ISBN: 978-1-0880-2302-0

10 9 8 7 6 5 4 3 2 1

EMPIRE PUBLISHING
www.empirebookpublishing.com

# Contents

**CHAPTER 1**
Drummer Boy ................................................................. 1

**CHAPTER 2**
I Got Him ...................................................................... 10

**CHAPTER 3**
My First Love ............................................................... 19

**CHAPTER 4**
Alone In Marriage ....................................................... 33

**CHAPTER 5**
How I Got Out .............................................................. 39

**CHAPTER 6**
Mind Control ................................................................ 45

**CHAPTER 7**
Hello, Sin City .............................................................. 50

**CHAPTER 8**
The Call Girl Who Was Never Called ...................... 54

**CHAPTER 9**
How Low Can You Go? .............................................. 62

**CHAPTER 10**
Church Hurt and Compromised ............................... 70

**CHAPTER 11**
Finding My Worth and My Happily Ever After ................ 86

# INTRODUCTION

I never thought I would find myself this hurt, this broken. No one told me that giving my heart to someone would be me risking the possibility of it being broken. And OH, was I broken! I never felt a hurt like this before, and because I was hurting so bad, I blacked out and all I saw was rage. So I shot him! Yes, that's right! Shot him twice! Once in his back and the other in his leg. And the only reason why I hit his leg is because he ran and I missed. I was actually going for a deadly shot, SUCKA! I wanted him to suffer just like he made me suffer. So after I shot him, I walked into the kitchen to grab some of my favorite ingredients. Then on my way out the door, I stepped over him. He was weeping like a little baby! I should have known he was a punk! "What? Can't take a bullet!?" Out the house I went. I busted out his car windows, flattened his tires, poured sugar and syrup in his gas tank, and cement sealed his car doors shut. Don't ask where I got the cement from. I was determined he was gone pay for what he did to me!

But once I was done daydreaming about what I wanted to do to him, I decided to pack my stuff and leave just like I was asked to. HA! It was clear this chapter of my life was pretty much over. But I knew I had a long way to go. I also knew that I was hurting, full of rage with a desire for revenge and that eventually; I would have to revisit this place so I can heal from it all. So here it is… BUT wait! First, let me take you back to the year 2001… because that is where it all started for me.

# CHAPTER 1

## Drummer Boy

When I was sixteen years old, this guy came to the church my mother and I were attending at the time. Come to find out, he was our new drummer and I found him to be pretty cute. He had his own car, so I assumed he had to be older than me. After him being a part of the church for a while and attending a few choir rehearsals, he finally decided to speak to me. Just general conversation; nothing major…Yet. So we decided to exchange numbers. No harm in that, right? It was a cloudy day in sunny San Diego, California, and I decided to give him a call. Surprisingly, he answered! He was out and about driving. We had a long conversation that day; I'm talking hours. That's when your phone battery lasted about two days without you plugging it in to be charged. All we did was talk and text for hours every day, and one day he asked me out on a date. And of course, I accepted his invitation. He picked me up and we went to the movies. We had a ball. That was my first real date; well, outside of my dad taking me and my sister on dates when we were younger. This guy was funny, goofy, and very charming. He was also a gentleman and very sweet. If he asked, I would definitely go on another date with him. He took me home right after the movies. He didn't try anything like a young man probably would have and probably should have. I mean, I was cute, so I expected him to try everything, but he didn't which was surprising.

He walked me to the door; it was about 9 pm and I was feeling myself, and him of course, so I told him to come back later that night once my parents went to bed. Yeah, you know what that mean... Let's just say, that was the night I experienced my very first orgasm, which is probably the only reason he made it in this book.

Anyway, after that night, that man had my heart. That's also the night I probably became one of the dumbest young girls on the planet. Everything was great for about three months, then it all went downhill from there. He started to spend less and less time with me unless it was church.

He wouldn't answer my phone calls at certain times when previously he would always answer my calls. I started to see an aggressive side of him. Going into about our fourth month of being an official couple, we stayed off and on for weeks at a time. On one week, and off another. When he would get mad, he would be very aggressive, even so much to the point that one day he put his hands on me! And not just in any kind of way; he punched me in the face! My eye to be exact! Of course, I punched him back because I have never been known not to fight back. So needless to say, there I was with a bruised eye. I tried to cover it up because how do you explain to your parents, or even your teachers (because I was still in high school) for that matter that your boyfriend had punched you in the face?

When my mother saw my face, she asked me what happened. I told her that I got into a fight at school with some girls that were trying to jump me, and that took care of that. So after everything this man child had done so far, you would have thought that I would be done, right? Yeah, I should have been done but my dumb behind went right back to him. Crazy, right!?

We were good for about a week after the altercation. I hadn't been arguing or fighting with him, so things were good between us. Then Sunday comes. And this man child had done the imaginable. He showed up to church with another girl! Yes, this man was that bold and heartless that he came to church with another woman. She was a beautiful girl too! And seemed to be very nice. Needless to say, I was HOT, and of course was wondering who she was the entire service. When service was over, I started to make my way over toward him so I could introduce myself. He started to walk out the door, heading toward the parking lot of the church. I followed behind him because I needed answers. He turned around because he forgot something in the church.

He started walking back towards me, and once he got close enough to me, I thought he was going to stop and talk to me, and of course explain himself, right!? NOPE! He said, "Hi," and kept walking. At that point, I was shocked and stuck that this was even happening to me. So, I waited there in the parking lot for my mother to come out so we could go home. I was furious! Smoking HOT. I didn't want to make a scene because one, we were at church. Two, I didn't want to embarrass my mother, and three, I didn't want to look like the typical "jealous, crazy chick"; even though deep down inside, I was. He walked past me again and didn't say anything. I just watched him as he walked over to his car. He opened the car door for her and she got in. As he closed her door, he waved at me, hopped in the driver seat, and sped off!

I called him the next day and we argued about it. He apologized and told me she was just a member of another church that he played the drums for. Of course, I didn't believe him, but I wanted to believe him. And because I wanted to believe him, we were back at it. More ups and downs, more fights, more abuse. Crazy, right? I knew that I didn't deserve what I was experiencing from this young man. Especially not at the age of 16. I didn't grow up like that, and I definitely wasn't raised like that. But I couldn't help but think about what took place at the church. How what he did kept replaying in my head. Every time I thought about it and pictured what he did to me, I got mad all over again. So I came up with an idea… I decided that I was going to call the girl, but I didn't have her number and I didn't know anybody who knew her because I had never seen her before. I talked to my best friend about it at the time, and she came up with the best idea. She told me to get her number from his phone. I said to my friend, "How will I know who she is? I don't even know the girl's name." She said, "Look through his text messages and his call log to see who he's frequently talking to." I said, "You're right!" That's exactly what I decided to do. Also, I thought it would be smart that while I grabbed the number, to also look for text messages between them.

One afternoon, we were hanging out and he fell asleep. As soon as I saw that he was pretty deep in his slumber, I crept over, grabbed his phone, and got the girl's number.

I didn't call her that same day. I waited until later in the week because I did not want to call her by myself. I wanted my best friend present. One day after school, I decided it was the day that I was going to call that girl and get my answers! My best friend and I talked about it the whole school bus ride home (Isn't that crazy!? It even sounds weird as I'm writing this that I was dealing with adult things in high school). We made it to the house and got settled. We sat on the couch and I was nervous as all get out, because I had never done a thing like that before. I picked up the phone, hit *67 to block my number (y'all remember that, right?), and there it was, the phone started ringing. I had it on speaker so my best friend could hear as well. The phone was still ringing, and after the fourth ring, she answered! I was nervous and shocked that she even picked up. She answered, and I told her who I was, and who I was calling about which was my boyfriend, and that I wanted her to answer some questions for me. She replied, "Ok." I asked her if she was dating him. She said yes. I asked her how long they had been dating. She told me that they had been dating for a few months. I started to feel myself get angry, but I kept my cool for the sake of not looking crazy. I think it was kind of too late for that because I had already called the girl.

I proceeded to ask her my second question of which I was not ready to hear the answer, but I asked anyway. I asked, "Are you guys having sex?" She replied, "Yes, we are." My heart immediately dropped, and because I was overwhelmed with feelings and emotions, the only thing I could do was hang up on her. I didn't understand why I hung up on the girl because she was so sweet and innocent. She wasn't hostile with me and she didn't catch an attitude with me. She was very calm in her responses to me. I was the rude one. I guess I didn't want to believe it. I did not call her back. I was embarrassed, ashamed, and hurt. To be honest, there was nothing else for us to discuss. She answered all my questions. I didn't need to know anything else.

From that moment forward, I knew I could not be with him anymore, so I cut him off. I didn't answer his phone calls. I just texted him and told him, "I know about your new girlfriend. I called her and spoke with her, and she confirmed that you guys are indeed dating. I am done with you! Don't call me, don't text me, don't reach out to me. We are done!"

I moved on with my life. It hurt of course, but I had other things to focus on, such as graduating from high school, living my life as a 16, soon-to-be 17-year-old. I wanted to enjoy hanging out with my friends and discovering who I was.

About three months goes by and there was this youth explosion at a pretty popular church in town where I was praise dancing and singing. And of course, I ran into him. We didn't have any words for each other; there was nothing to say to him. When he saw me, he kind of stopped and looked because I was looking pretty fly. Your girl was a cute little something back then. I kept walking, and shortly after I saw him, I saw her and she was pregnant! I mean pregnant with a huge belly pregnant! Surprisingly, it broke my heart. Even though we weren't together anymore and I had moved on, it still hurt to see her with his child. To feel those feelings after months of not dealing with him or seeing him was a very weird feeling. A part of me was saying, well, you still love him, and another part of me was saying, it's wrong to feel that way about him.

What I have learned is that both feelings are ok. You have to process things effectively. Just because you cut someone out of your life and choose not to deal with them anymore doesn't mean the feelings leave. Those feelings will stick around until you get over it and move on from them. Now, how do you move on from them?

• Be honest with how you feel. Don't lie to yourself because if you claim to be in a space that you're not, you're deceiving yourself, and moving on will never be effective. You'll move on out of hurt, anger, and lack thereof; which is not moving on.

• Process those feelings, identify them and replace them with positive things. For example, for the words, "He hurt me," alter with, "I don't deserve to be hurt but loved the right way." As you continue to speak those positive things to void out those negative things, you will become stronger and began to see your self-worth.

- Also, you'll be able to see that he/she wasn't for you, and you will be glad that you got out of that toxic relationship.

That chapter is closed…

# CHAPTER 2

## I Got Him

After the entanglement with the drummer boy, I didn't want anything to do with relationships. I was not looking to get involved or to be with anybody. I started focusing on myself, my academics, and being happy. Enjoying my friends and the life a young teenage girl should enjoy. One day a friend of mine came to me. She knew a lady who wrote a movie and was looking for actors to fill different roles. And she remembered that I was an actress. I loved acting. My mother introduced me to acting when I was 6 years old. I started out with commercials such as Mossy Nissan and Oscar Mayer, just to name a couple. I then went on to movies such as *The Little Rascals* and *Posy Does No Homework*, which was later changed to *Dangerous Minds*. I also acted in *Sister Act 2*, and a handful of some of America's favorite TV shows.

Being a child actor can be challenging. In order for me to continue in that career path as a young actress, one of the main requirements was that I had to keep my grades up in school. If they dropped below average, I would have to turn down anything that was offered to me until the following grade period to see if I made any improvements. Well, needless to say, I never brought my grades back up. At least not until I actually hit grade school. Which is pretty sad to say because had I continued on that path, there is no telling where I could have been today. But I always knew I belonged on the big screen as they would call it. So even up to this point, I've always remained hopeful.

My friend asked me if I would be interested in the opportunity. I told her that I would and asked her to get back to me with all the details. I informed her that I would need to swing it by my mom and let her know. The very next day, she came to me with all the information concerning the movie; audition dates, times of filming, etc. I took it home to my mother and she approved it. The audition was taking place during the weekend which was approaching fast, just two days out to be exact. Finally, the weekend came and my audition was the next day, which was a Saturday. My friend and I decided to ride together, because she knew where the place was and she also knew the lady. Plus, my mom wasn't available to take me because she was getting her hair done. And you know back then, when you went to the salon to get your hair done, that was an all-day trip. So her mother agreed to take us both to the audition. She picked me up on the way there. The whole time in the car, I was thinking of the possibilities of what could come of the opportunity. I was excited and ready to audition. We finally arrived to our destination and her mother dropped us off because she had somewhere else to be. She told us to call when we were ready. My friend and I thanked her for driving us to the audition.

We got out the car to head inside the building where the auditions were being held. It wasn't the best of buildings. You could tell it was a community theater. But hey, I wasn't tripping; I was just excited. We walked in and there were a few people waiting for the auditions to start; about three girls and two other guys. One, who was tall, dark, and handsome; I later found out he was a very close friend of my family. So over the course of us practicing for this "movie," he became like a brother to me. He called me his little sister.

Even till this day, we will shoot a quick message to each other over social media every now and then, just to check to see how each other is doing.

My friend and I took a seat where the other actors were sitting, and we began to introduce ourselves to them and make conversation until it was time for the auditions to start. While we were talking, this light-skinned man walked through the door, who was amazingly handsome and nicely presentable; he had so much swag.

He came in pretty quick and to himself. He did come over to where we were sitting and asked us if he was at the audition for the movie; he said the name of the movie. We told him that he was at the right place. He said, "Cool," and walked back over to where he was sitting.

By this time, auditions were starting. The person who wrote the movie script went up on stage to properly introduce herself and explained the movie and its purpose. Shortly after her introduction, she began to call people up one by one to read their desired parts. And for some, after they read the lines of the character they chose themselves, she would have them read the lines of the character that she thought would best fit them.

Then it was my turn! The character I chose to audition for was the girlfriend of the main character. I began reading. I was nervous but I thought I was doing pretty well. After I was done, she asked me to read another character, which was a Jamaican woman with an accent. She asked me if I could speak with a Jamaican accent. I say, "Yes, I think I can." Surprisingly, British and Jamaican accents are something I can do easily.

I read that role and blew it out of the water. She loved it and so did everyone else by their responses.

After everyone had gone, she got up and said, "I thought it would take a few days, but I believe I have my actors for my film. If I call your name, stay. If I don't, thank you for your time." You could tell everyone became nervous and anxious. She began to call out names and people were cheering as she continued. I was also cheering, in hopes to be picked as well. I saw about five people get called, and still, my name has not been mentioned. Even light skin got called. I was happy for him. But I started to worry because she hadn't said my name. Lo and behold, I was last on the list to be called. I was so relieved and excited!

The people that weren't called had left, and it was just seven of us that remained. We congratulated each other and sat there for another hour just talking and getting to know each other as cast members. We wanted to build a bond and chemistry, so when we filmed, it would be all natural. This was one of the best days of my life. Definitely a day to remember. On the way out the building, we were all walking and talking, getting ready to leave, and I looked over to see my friend that I came with chopping it up with light skin by his car. Everyone started to leave little by little, and I was pretty much waiting for our ride to pick us up. I saw their conversation wrap up and he got in his car. She began to walk toward me. As she was walking, she said to me, "He's going to give us a ride home." I asked if she was sure and she said yes. I asked her if she called her mother to tell her not to come pick us up. Look at me trying to be responsible. She said yes, so I headed across the parking lot to get in the car. He had a nice medium-size SUV; clean on the inside. I'm an observer. So I pretty much notice everything. I may not say anything about it, but I see it.

She hopped in the front seat. I was in the back sitting behind him. He asked me what part of town I stayed in so he could start heading that way. I told him what direction to go in and we pulled off. On the way home, he and my friend were talking while I listened. I was thinking, *she moves pretty fast.* I thought when I saw her talking to him back in the parking lot that she may have known him or something. But as I was listening to their conversation, they didn't know each other at all. But it was clear they wanted to. So, I remained quiet and allowed her to do her thing. I'm not one to block anything. I wasn't that type of friend. We arrived at my house and I thanked him for the ride. I told my friend to call me once she got home. Isn't it crazy!? Only 16/17 years old and operating like we were adults. Man, I tell you, we were fast young girls. I watched them pull off as I headed in the house. I was wondering if she would even make it home; wondering if she would text me. Well, needless to say, she never did. She instead called me once she got in the house. She shared with me in excitement how she was really feeling light skin, and how he seemed so amazing, and of course, how FINE he was! I was excited for her. I told her he was very cute. I also told her to be careful. She said, "Of course!" She finished sharing how amazing he was, and shortly after, we called it a night. I had to get up for church in the morning.

That Monday hit, which was the beginning of a new school week, yippie! Can you hear my enthusiasm to get up and go to school? Anyway, I was able to find some type of joy concerning the day because it was also the day of our first official rehearsal for the movie. I was excited to meet up with the cast members again. My friend and I had come up with a plan to get to our rehearsals from school. Our school was very far out from where we lived and of course we were able to take the school bus, but we weren't going home. We decided to take the city bus which we could catch right in front of our high school. Our rehearsals were in downtown San Diego. The city bus would take us up about a block from where we had to be. So we would just hop off the bus and walk down the block every day we had rehearsals.

About a week went by of this new routine and rehearsals. And everything was going. Filming was going great, and the cast members were fun to be around. And I felt like I was in my true element. It seemed like my friend and light skin were getting along pretty good, until I noticed things began to shift with him. I mean, not in a bad way. Well, at least I didn't view it as bad at the time. The shift was his sudden focus and interest in me. He started to talk to me more and go out of his way to speak to me. I didn't think anything of it until one day at rehearsal. Every time I looked up or around, I caught him staring at me! This was weird and uncomfortable for me because I would always think to myself, during and after rehearsals, *if he's interested in my friend, why do I catch him looking at me all the time*? That's because he was no longer interested in my friend. He wanted me! He even went as far as flirting with me in front of her, which was rude and made me feel uncomfortable. But I'm not gone lie. It felt good to be wanted. And semi-chased. It was the first time I had ever experienced being pursued by a man, even though it wasn't formal or traditional at the moment, because he was talking to my friend. And I say man because he was 20 years old. I was 17 with a birthday in a few months. I was never disrespectful to my friend by trying to talk to him nor did I go behind her back with any funny business. Their relationship naturally shifted. One day she came up to me right before rehearsal started. She said she wanted to talk, so we go down the hall, away from our rehearsal area. She said, "I can tell he likes you. It's pretty obvious." I looked at her with a shocked face because I was not expecting her to say that to me. She asked, "Do you like him too?" I was afraid to answer because I didn't want her to be mad at me, nor did I want to hurt her feelings. But I knew I had to be honest with her. I replied, "I do like him." She responded, "It's ok, you guys would be great together." Jumping for joy on the inside... *You mean I get to keep my friend and get the guy?* Talk about a mature moment. That was very adult of her. She hugged me afterwards and we headed back into rehearsal. From that day forward, he didn't know what she and I discussed. And it didn't matter. Because as soon as she gave me the green light to be with him, it was like we became magnets, and surprisingly, it was a smooth transition. That was one of the most refreshing moments of my life. And I wouldn't change any of it if I had the opportunity to do it all over again. He was perfect. We were perfect, and it was exactly what I needed after a devastating heartbreak. This man was a breath of fresh air. And the most important part about it all? It was real! What we felt for each other was real. I'm not talking puppy love. We knew that what we had was serious. Because you could feel it. He was my beginning to a new world, a new me, and a new love.

# CHAPTER 3

## My First Love

There I was, with the man of my dreams, the man I knew I would spend the rest of my life with. We both knew that we wanted to be with each other for life. We were just too young to act upon it. I mean, I was still in high school. His courtship was perfect. He was the ultimate gentleman. He would open up doors for me. Buy me things. Bring me flowers. When he would go buy himself shoes, he would buy me a matching pair so we could be the cute matching couple. Y'all know how it go. And that was everything back in the early/mid 2000s. We met each other's parents. They all approved of us. It was perfect. He even joined the church that I was a member of. We did ministry together. There we were, a young, and I mean very young saved couple. Trying to be a good example of living right before God. And as if that wasn't hard enough for us, we were also practicing abstinence. You know, NO SEX BEFORE MARRIAGE? Yes, that! Boy, was it hard! Especially because we were both extremely attracted to each other. When he hugged me, I would melt! And I'm not even going to tell you what his kisses did to me. So, you can imagine the urge to rip his clothes off. But we restrained ourselves… until one late afternoon. He picked me up from school and took me home. We arrived to the house and both of my parents were at work.

We went in, I put my book bag down, and we went to the kitchen to grab something to drink. You know, typical things. We took a seat on the couch and stated talking, just conversing about the day we both had. I leaned in to kiss him. And that's how it all started. We were kissing and he started rubbing all over my body. I was doing the same with him, and before I knew it, we were upstairs in my parents' room! Don't ask me why we didn't go to my room. Maybe because when you're a teenager, having sex in your parents' or momma's room was better than having sex in yours. I don't know. Or maybe it was just me. I began to take my clothes off, and he looked at me like, *I can't believe this is happening.* In my mind, I was thinking the same thing. Like, *am I really going to do this*? My pants came off. I said *YEP! I'm doing it!* By this time, he had his clothes off as well. I laid on the bed, and we got to it! I could not believe that we were doing something we had promised and committed not to do. The whole time, although it felt good and it's what my body had been craving, I couldn't enjoy it because conviction was eating me up! So I said, "Stop! Let's stop! We can't keep going. This is bad and not what we agreed upon." And because I was immature and didn't know how to effectively process what I was feeling, which was disappointment, conviction, defeat, and failure, I broke up with him. Yes, broke up with him while he was standing there butt naked. I told him, "If we slept together before marriage, we can no longer be together." Isn't that crazy?! I was willing to throw away the whole relationship with this great guy because we slept together. I told you I was immature. So we both got dressed. I wasn't mad at him, and I didn't speak in an angry tone. I was hurt and felt bad about what I did. And so did he. His words were few. He let himself out of the house and left. I laid in my bed crying as he left because my feelings were hurt that I messed up and that I broke up with him. About 20 minutes later, I heard my mother come in the house. I got up, dried my eyes, and walked out of my room to say hi to her. I got to the stairs and she was standing there with him. I was confused because I was thinking, *what is he still doing here? He was supposed to leave. And why did he come in with my mother? That's weird.* My mother told him to stay by the door. She started walking up the stairs to me and told me to go to my room. I was like, WHAT IS GOING ON!? I thought to myself, *you're in trouble now!* We went in the room and she closed the door. She said, "He told me what happened." I looked at her with a puzzled look but was screaming on the inside. She said, "And I saw him crying about to get in his car when I pulled up in the driveway. So I got out of the car and stopped him to find out what happened. And he told me because he was so hurt, and he didn't want to break up with you." My mom didn't tell me whether to break up with him or not. She just gave me a little wisdom and told me, "It's your choice." By the time she was done talking to me which was about five minutes, I made the decision to not break up with him. I walked out the room and saw him still standing at the bottom of the stairs waiting for whatever was going to happen. I began to walk down toward him and he met me at the second to last step. He grabbed my hand and told me, "I don't want to break up with you. I'm sorry. I love you." I was in shock and awe of his sentiments and expression toward me. I told him, "I'm not breaking up with you, baby. I love you too." From that day forward, it was on and poppin! We were living life, enjoying each other and humping like rabbits. Hey, the door was open; no sense of shutting it. We were happy. We were going to church, and shortly after that, he became our pastor's armor bearer. Our pastor just so happened to be a pretty successful and well-known gospel artist. So he would travel with him a lot, and I was even afforded the opportunity to tag along on a few occasions. It was a pretty dope experience. Especially at the age of 19! Because by this time, I had graduated high school and didn't have any real obligations, so I was able to pretty much go and come as I pleased. Of course, with responsibility of still checking in with my mother and letting her know my whereabouts and things like that. I spent a lot of my time at church or was always doing things with church friends and family, so she was ok with it all.

Then something happened to me that would change my world forever. I found out that I was PREGNANT. Yes, at the age of 19, pregnant with my first child! I couldn't believe it. I was so scared and unsure about it all. So I called my sister/friend from church to tell her I needed her to get to my house quickly because something happened. Of course, she asked me what happened, and told me that I was scaring her a little. She told me that she would be on the way in a few minutes. We hung up and I was just sitting at home in my bathroom, stuck, in disbelief. *This can't be happening to me. I'm enjoying life right now.* Clearly, a little too much enjoyment, right?! I was thinking, what will my mother say to me? My dad? Although, he wasn't in the house anymore because he and my mother were getting a divorce. But that is another story for another time. I'm sure he would have still been disappointed that his daughter was pregnant. And not even 21 yet. After drowning myself in my thoughts and sorrow, the doorbell rang, and it was my sister/friend. I ran downstairs to open the door and she said, "Girl, what's the problem? You had me flying on the freeway!" I reached behind me to grab the pregnancy test out of my back pocket. I handed it to her and said, "Look." She said, "Oh wowzers," then proceeds to say, "This is what you had me come over for? You could have told me this over the phone!" And she chuckled a little. Needless to say, she wasn't that surprised or shocked by it. She was about 27 with two beautiful little girls. She was already a mother. She said, "Well, welcome to the club, girl." I was looking at her like, *shut up! You make me sick!* We sat down and talked about it. She asked me how I felt about it all. And I shared with her my feelings about it. But what I really needed was a plan on how I was going to break the news to my mother. That was my concern at the time. I guess most people tell the baby daddy first. Not me! She said, "If you want, I could be here when you tell her so you don't have to do it alone." I said, "Yes! That would be good, and will make me feel a little more comfortable." She said, "Ok, when do you want to tell her?" I said, "I will let you know. I have to process this for myself." She said, "Ok. Well, just call me and I'll come over when you are ready." She left after that. Over the next few days, I wallowed in my thoughts. As I was thinking about everything, I decided to have my

Godmother come over when I told my mother rather than my sister/friend. Nothing against her. For some reason, with any major event in my life, I would always call my Godmother. Even until this day, it's the same thing. Which is weird and not necessarily done on purpose, but that's just the way it was and had been. Maybe I should change that!

I gave my Godmother a call, and I tell her everything. She was always so calm, and it was like nothing ever shocked her. I asked her if she could be present when I broke the news to my mother. She agreed. She asked, "You want me to come over tomorrow after I get out of work?" I take a deep break and reply, "Yes, please." I tell her thank you and she said, "This why I'm here! You're welcome. See you tomorrow." We hang up and I'm nervous as ever! Knowing the next day I would tell my mother that I was pregnant! It was something I thought I wouldn't have to do for a while. Years to come. But NO, this was my reality and there was no changing it. The following day, I woke up with the heaviness of the information that I was carrying. I was honestly a little happy about telling my mother because now I could relieve myself of the secret I had been carrying over the past few days.

I got myself up, showered, got dressed, fixed me something to eat, and just relaxed until my Godmother got off work. My mother came home from work and yelled, "Hey!" I said hey back! She headed upstairs to get settled in. About two hours after that, my Godmother texted me to tell me she was on her way over. I immediately felt this gut-wrenching feeling. And my nerves began to creep in all over again. I didn't let it get the best of me though. My Godmother arrived, and by that time, my mother was in the kitchen cooking. So we met her in the kitchen. She saw my Godmother walk in behind me and they greeted and hugged each other. My mother asked my Godmother, "What are you doing here?" *Oh Lord, the magic question!* My Godmother replied, "We have to talk to you." My mother said, "Ok, let me turn my fire off and take this out the pot first." Godmother said, "We'll be in the living room." We walked out the kitchen into the living room and took a seat. My mom came in shortly after and had a seat with us. My mother said, "Ok, I'm ready. What's up?" My Godmother said, "Kellie has something to say." My mother looked at me in anticipation. Of course, I paused and took a deep breath. Then I said to her, "I'm pregnant. I had Godmomma come over because I did not want to tell you by myself." My mom said, "I knew it! I knew you were pregnant because over the past few days you didn't eat breakfast when you always eat breakfast." She told me that she wasn't mad or upset. Just a little disappointed because I was still young, and I still had my whole life ahead of me. She told me that she loved me and that she would help support me.

I was shocked! I didn't see it happening that way. But I was grateful. And even more grateful that I had supportive people around me.

But it's unfortunate that I could not say the same about my boyfriend/baby daddy. When I broke the news to him, he told me that he didn't want me to have the baby. Not because of me necessarily, but because he already had a daughter who was almost 4 years old at the time. And he didn't want any more children at that time. My response to him was, "I'm going to have this baby with or without you. So whatever you gotta do or feel that you need to do, go ahead and do it. Because me and this baby will be alright." He got up and left. When he walked out that door, I didn't know what to expect from him. But one thing I did know is that certain situations can bring out the ugly in people. So I prepared myself for the worst, just in case.

He didn't talk to me for about a week. And then on a Saturday morning, my phone rang. It was him! I looked at my screen for a few rings because I didn't know if he was calling me on some foolishness or calling me because he came to his right mind. I answered after a few rings and he greeted me. I replied, "What's up?" with a very uninterested tone. He said, "I was calling because I wanted to apologize about the other day, and what I said. I was in my feelings and didn't even consider your feelings about the whole thing. It was wrong of me. I want you to know that I'm here with and for you. And I will support you through it."

I was in shock of what my ears had just heard. I wasn't expecting a phone call from him, let alone for him to say those things to me. I was quiet for about 10 seconds and he said, "Hello?" I replied, "Yes, I'm still here. Thank you for deciding to be here for me. It's a relief to know that I can count on the father of my future child to be here and support me." He said, "Well, I was never NOT going to be here. It was just a matter of us being together if anything. But I still would have taken care of my responsibilities as a father. Whether I wanted the baby or not. I'm no deadbeat dad." We continued talking and made up over the phone. Now everything was good. We began to share the news with family, friends, and extended loved ones. We became excited to plan our new life as first-time parents. Well, him, not so much. But me? I'll be a new mommy of a precious new baby. Oh, if it's a boy, it would be what I prayed and hoped for. A few months passed by and I was about five months pregnant. My belly was showing really good. My due date was May 23rd, 2007. It was January 10th on a Sunday afternoon. My child's father and I had just come in from church. He said he had to run an errand really quickly and that he would be back within the hour. I said, "Ok, no problem. On your way back, can you please stop and grab me something to eat?" He said, "Sure! Text me what you want." He gave me a kiss and ran out the door. I was big and round so I went to have myself a seat! I was breathing hard and having hot flashes. As soon as I flopped down on the couch and caught my breath, I felt myself falling to sleep. But I hadn't changed my clothes yet. So I sat there for another 20 minutes talking, trying to talk myself into getting up off the couch to change my clothes. The struggle was serious, y'all. By this time, 40 minutes had gone by. And before I knew it, he was back. I knew because I heard his car pull up in the driveway. I said to myself, *man, you have to get up now and open the door for him.* So I slid up; yes, you read right, slid up and scooted myself off the couch to get to that door for him. I opened the door and he walked in with flowers and handed them to me. I closed the door and said with a smile, "Awe baby, thank you." He began to express his feelings and emotions toward me. He told me how much he loved me and while he was talking, he reached into his back pocket and pulled out a little black box. My heart began to race, and he dropped down on one knee, opened the box, and it was a beautiful diamond ring. He said, "Will you marry me?" I stood there in utter shock and overjoyed with my mouth wide open! I uttered the words, "Yes, yes, yes!" He put the ring on my finger and jumped up to kiss me. "Can you believe I'm engaged! Wow!" I said to my mother. She was excited about it. She also thought I was a little too young to be engaged. But for the most part, she was excited for us. We planned to have a big wedding after I had the baby. Well, sadly, that never happened. I had the baby, and he was gorgeous; 6lb 14oz, 20inch to be exact! After having the baby, our relationship slowly went downhill. No, he didn't cheat; neither did I. He was just comfortable in our relationship. There wasn't anything particularly wrong. He was still very sweet; a gentleman, definitely a great dad. He just became content where we were. And I wanted more. I asked him to revisit this wedding so we could be married and do the right thing before God. And these were his words verbatim, "I'm ok with where we are right now. I don't want to move forward yet." Hearing those words hurt me. I asked him, "Why don't you want to move forward with me?" His response was, "I'm just not ready." I couldn't believe it. *This is the man I've spent the last three and a half years with. This is the man I had my first baby with. This is my first true love.* But quickly after all these things ran through my mind so fast like lightning, I stopped and heard a small still voice that said, "Wrong, God is your first true love."

I was a little scared because that had never happened to me before. I thought I was hearing things! Until I heard the small still voice again say, "Let it go." I knew then that I wasn't hearing things. And this extreme confidence and boldness came out of nowhere, and I said to him, "Well, we can't continue with our relationship. We must continue to grow, and if we're not growing, we're dying. By you being content that means to me that we are not growing. So I'm calling it quits." And you know what his reply was? "Ok." This negro didn't even put up a fight or rebuttal; nothing! This confirmed to me his reason for not wanting to move forward. Even though it hurt me, and I mean hurt bad, I was ok with walking away from him. Because I knew that I deserved more.

**Steps:**

1: Ladies, I must let you know; you are worth it, you are worth it, you are worth it. Know it, own it. And don't go back on it. And repeat it as many times as you need to. Until it sinks in and you begin to believe it. And most importantly, say it until your actions produce it.

2: When you have been with a man for years or you guys have children together, and you bring up marriage, and he tells you "not yet," then you make it your business to ask him "why not?" Be sure to get to the bottom of the matter. It's ok to apply pressure on him, and if he's a good man, and you're the right woman, he won't crack under the pressure. He will get himself ready, even when he feels he's not ready. Because he will deem you worth it.

Speaking of marriage... it was clear that I was not ready for what was about to come next in my life. And I don't think you're ready either! As you turn the page, hold on, because this is about to get a little rocky.

# CHAPTER 4
## Alone In Marriage

Have you ever wondered why it's so easy to lose who you are when in relationships? I'm sure a lot of us haven't because when you lose who you are or get off track of what you're supposed to be pursuing in life, we typically don't realize it. We don't notice we are off life's course concerning us. All we know is what's right in front of us... and that's either happiness, hurt, or disappointment...or all three for that matter.

I know because I was way off, but I didn't realize it until I got married. Let me take you into the short journey of the matrimony that would soon be my worst nightmare.

Here I am at 22 years old; with one child from a previous relationship and one on the way. Yes, I said it! I was marrying the man of my dreams, not knowing me marrying him would distract me from my dreams. You're probably wondering what I mean by that, right? Well, we got married because I was pregnant with his child and for other beneficial reasons of course, which was wrong to begin with. You never marry someone because you have a child with them. I regretfully learned the hard way that being a parent and life partner are two different things and commitments. So, we mustn't mix the two. Just because someone makes a great parent does not mean they will make a great spouse. We have to keep things in the right perspective.

So not only was I getting married, I was pregnant and had a child from my previous relationship. I was totally off life's course of where I should have been. I was distracted from what I should have done and should have been doing. And most importantly, I lost who I was. The craziest part about that is, I didn't even know it. Different things that happened to me over the years, things that I have gone through, different decisions I have made, turned me into this woman who was in need of a revival and direction. I got caught up in what was now my new normal, my life as a mother and a wife; which I knew nothing about other than what I saw my mother do. But yet and still, I had to figure it out for me and my marriage.

And let me tell you, my marriage went bad very quickly, but what did I expect? When my reason behind getting married was wrong to begin with. And in the middle of all of this, I was still trying to figure out who I was and what I was supposed to be doing in life. However, I didn't realize I was far from that person. She was buried under wife, mother, failure, underachiever, liar, and the list goes on.

But what I want my single folks to know (first, if you're not married, you are single):

- *Before you enter into any committed relationship, make sure you are happy with who you are, and who you are working toward becoming. And that is ranging from your physical appearance to your career. It's no one else's job to make you happy with who you are. That is your sole responsibility.*

- *Know who you are. Know what you like and don't like. What you want and don't want. And most importantly, what you don't want to deal with.*

- *And don't be afraid to say No. If you're just starting to date that person, don't be afraid to tell them they're not a match for you. It's ok that you are not compatible with that individual. We often try to make people fit our lives. We adjust our desires or standards all because we want so bad for that person to be the one for us. Don't do it! He is not the only man and she is not the only woman that is worthy of your time and heart. Like the old saying, there are other fish in the sea. Just be sure to launch into the deep. Because that's where you'll find bigger and quality fish.*

## "For my married people"

- *If you find yourself irritated with life, your spouse, feeling like you need more and or should be doing more with your life than what you are already doing, or maybe you are just unhappy, it's not that your life is bad, you just know that there's more you could be accomplishing.*

  *You first have to get back to the basics of who you are. What does that mean?*

  *Who were you before you got married?*

  *What did you like doing?*

  *What were you good at?*

  *All these things will help you spark and revitalize who you are and what you're supposed to be doing. Whether it's something you must let go or gain.*

- *If you never knew who you were, then I encourage you to get to know who God is because in him, you will find your identity.*

These steps are important to finding who you are so you mustn't skip them. But apply each one and watch things begin to change.

For me, it wasn't until I received a phone call from someone asking me to provide a service for them that

I used to do. Not only that but what I forgot I knew how to do. And very good at it too if I may add. That's when I said to myself, "Oh yeah, I am good at that," and from that day forward, I started to remember everything I used to do. I used to do hair, dance hip hop, I was an actress, I used to sing! Tell me, how does one forget they know how to sing? And just think, it's all because I made a decision that took me off life's course. It only takes one bad decision to throw you off the path that God has for you.

I had to get back to all these things and who I once was, and that was not an easy thing to do. Let me tell you, I had everything fighting me. First, my body because I just had a baby and my body wasn't having it. My mind telling me I couldn't; "you're too old now and you can't pursue those things that you used to pursue because people with families and kids can't do those things. We have to get jobs, not go after your dreams."

Then I had my husband. Let's just say he wasn't the most supportive. Now he was always there to provide, but I knew his heart really wasn't there. So that hurt! But even in the middle of what I had going on, I knew I had to get back to the Kellie I once was. Because when I started pursuing those gifts and talents and just things that I loved to do, I felt good about myself. I had confidence again. I felt fresh like I got new beginning, and I felt like I was on the right track. It gave me so much life. For the first time in a long while, I smiled. Not because someone told a joke, but because I was finally finding me and my purpose.

I felt so good about myself. It had been so long since I felt good that I forgot what it felt like to have confidence and self-love, and just that joy of pursuing things that you love. It's a magical feeling. I knew this was something I had to do and keep up with because I owed it to myself. I had cut myself off from pursuing things I loved due to the choices I made. I knew this was a feeling I could not let go of again. So I got out!

1. What I want you to do is to first remember what it is that you used to do, whether it was dancing, cooking, counseling people, making furniture, whatever it was.

2. Most importantly, how did it make you feel doing it?

3. Take the first step in becoming active in those things again.

4. Lastly, don't get caught up on who's not there to help or support you. You got this!

# CHAPTER 5

## How I Got Out

What I can do is tell you this long story of how everything went down, about how ugly it was and how getting out was not easy at all, and how I never thought in a million years that a fight with someone I loved and was married to would be so ugly. But I'll save that for another time. What I will tell you is that amongst the other changes I was making with me pursuing what I used to love doing and getting my happiness back, I also had to make changes in my marriage and I did. So I found myself in divorce court! It was something I not only didn't want to happen but something I tried to avoid desperately. Let me explain to you how desperate I was.

After we got married, around the three-month mark into the marriage, I was five months pregnant. He told me he was no longer in love with me, so you can imagine what I was thinking to myself, right? *I sure wish he would have told me before I decided to have this baby.* Now that I'm much older and wiser now, I could see how he would think that he was no longer in love with me. Truth is, he was never in love with me. For lack of a better word, he was in "LUST WITH ME" and I don't blame him for it. He took me at face value, which is what a lot of us do; not understanding that face value will not keep a marriage alive.

So back to how desperate I was for my marriage to work out... The day he mentioned to me that he was no longer in love with me, I tried everything I knew to fix it and change it. I switched up my appearance thinking that it would make a difference. I started planning date nights with other married couples in hopes for us to be encouraged and work out our marriage. NOPE! It didn't work. Because I realized only one of us was really trying and putting forth maximum effort. That's where a lot of marriages/relationships fail because only one person or neither person is putting forth maximum effort on their end to make it work. He had checked out a long time ago. His heart, mind, and spirit had moved on from the marriage. He was only there physically and financially, and when I say physically, I mean just his presence in the home. There was no sex, no hugging, no touching; NOTHING! I tried so hard because I wanted to break the generational curses of both of our families. My parents after 27 years of being together were divorced. His parents after years of being together, divorced. And let me tell you, when my parents went through their divorce, it was an ugly process. You need to know that when you decide to divorce, the parents don't just break up, the whole family is broken up. And I didn't want that for myself or my babies. But I also did not want them growing up in an unhealthy home. So I had to make a decision and my decision was to GET OUT.

I remember that day so clearly, and that was probably the first time since going through the marriage that I went to God with my heart instead of my emotions. See, when you go to God with your heart, you get a different understanding on things. When you go to him in your emotions, you risk being blind to the facts, and my facts were that this man no longer wanted our marriage, and no matter how hard I tried, there was nothing I could do to make him want to stay.

This was something I had to come to grips with. Oh, and it hurt me. But because I went to God wanting his help and what he wanted for me, I was able to accept his will concerning my marriage. And even though I didn't want his will at that moment because that meant I would have to accept the truth about it all, on top of me being hurt and broken that my marriage was pretty much dead, I had peace that immediately came over me. I mean, that peace was so heavy that my whole body became still. But it was so confusing because in my mind, I'm supposed to be upset, angry, hurt, and feeling every emotion possible. But NO! As soon as I came to the realization and understanding that it was over, peace reaffirmed that everything was going to be ok. And I knew then, that was God giving me "peace in the midst of my storm," so I started preparing. Preparing to leave, preparing to GET OUT.

Ladies, when you are forced with the decision to leave or stay:

1. First, make sure you are assessing the problem and situation without your feelings and emotions. Because when you do, you can't see it clearly, and most importantly, they are unstable.

Example: have you ever gone to bed feeling some type of way? Whether mad or hurt, and wake up the next day feeling totally different? That's because at that time you were in your emotions, and it's never good to make a decision out of your emotions. You probably are asking, how do you do that? You focus more on the problems that have occurred or the damage that person has caused in the relationship and less on how it made you feel.

2. Second, I advise you to go to God concerning the issues and make sure you put yourself before him first by asking him what part you played in the

relationship going wrong. Often, we point fingers, and it's so easy to blame the other person, but you have to remember two people are in a relationship. So both of you are at fault for something going wrong, whether big or small. Either way, allow God to show you yourself and your wrong.

3. Third, if you do decide to go to God, make sure you are ready to hear what he has to say and are willing to follow whatever instructions he gives you.

4. Lastly, don't wait until things go bad or blow up in the relationship to do a self-assessment. Doing a monthly or even a weekly assessment concerning your attitude or how you handle situations will help prevent the relationship from going bad. And this doesn't just apply to relationships. A self-assessment can be applied in every area of your life; in your career, in how you interact with people, or if you're in a leadership role. Doing this weekly or monthly can and will help you to overcome those self-issues. It just depends on how bad you actually want to be free of yourself.

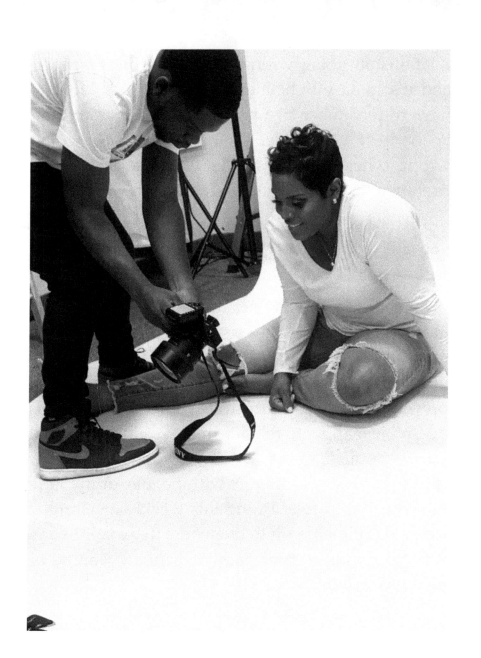

# CHAPTER 6

## Mind Control

Packing up myself and my children's things and leaving that house was devastating. Seeing our belongings in those boxes forced me to face my reality. And my reality was that I was 23 years old with two babies and a failed marriage.

Up to that point, those were the toughest and darkest times of my life. And the reason being is because for the first time, I realized I could not change what was happening. I had no control, and I could not take back what was said or done. I couldn't change his heart toward me, and I couldn't change any of the damage that had been done. I do believe that sometimes in certain situations, a lot of our hurt concerning failed relationships and marriages comes from the truth and reality that we don't possess the power to change what is currently happening. That we can't skip past or escape the emotions, the hurt, and effects of what has failed or is failing. That's also how we can stay stuck in toxic, unhealthy relationships; because we think we have the ability to change a person and their heart. And let me be the person to tell you if you have not been told already, THAT IS NOT SO.

I left with my babies. We ended up staying with some family members for a while until I got some paperwork taken care of and my finances in order. Boy, was it a day-to-day struggle, physically and emotionally. Physically because I had a 2-year-old toddler, and a 3-month-old infant who I was breastfeeding. So that explains itself. I was drained emotionally because all I could think about was him, and the hurt, the wrong, the abandonment, and everything else I could think of that had been done to me. So when everyone would go to bed, I would cry myself to sleep, because I had to be superwoman during the day. No one would see me (especially my kids) crying or with my head hanging low.

But the craziest part about this is that after everything happened, the hurt and pain this man had caused me, I still desired to be with him. Can you believe I wanted to work it out with him? I was telling myself that it wasn't that bad, and he could change. No, he didn't love me the way that I needed to be loved but it's ok. I told myself that I wasn't a needy person, I didn't need him to love me properly, I loved myself, and that was enough! I didn't understand that if I loved myself the way that I should have, I wouldn't be willing to settle for less than what I deserved and expected. See, when you love yourself, you have expectations and standards. You won't settle being treated just any kind of way.

I realized I was going through a mind battle, and I was allowing my hurt to tell me lies and dictate my decisions. I knew that it was wrong for me to think the way I was thinking, but I couldn't help it. All I knew was that I had to change it. I couldn't stay in that state of mind.

I knew then that me getting out wasn't so much physically but mentally. There I was living somewhere else, not even married anymore. I moved on physically, but I never moved on in my mind. All I did was take that same situation to a new place.

I went in circles for years after I had moved away. Trying to figure out who I was again. I was having sex with different men that I wasn't in a relationship with. At one point, I even tried to be a prostitute, and I was a Christian, saved and filled with the Holy Ghost! I'm not going to get into all that. I'll save that story for some other time.

**But this is what I want you to know:**

1 When a relationship has turned upside down or has ended, don't think for one second that you have the ability to change that person. Only God can change the heart of someone.

2 It's ok to take the time to be hurt and broken. It's ok to cry, and it's ok to seek professional help if needed. Now, it's not ok to stay hurt and broken, but don't rush to be healthy. Because when you do, you don't heal properly. Not just that, you find yourself getting busy, trying to not feel. You begin filling voids, which leads to you building and developing this false sense of confidence and happiness.

Don't believe the lie. If you want to bounce back greater than who you were before you got into the mess, you have to take time to heal properly.

3. You deserve for someone to love you, beyond condition, beyond circumstances, beyond you! Don't settle for less than you deserve. And you deserve to be loved properly. But make sure you love yourself first.

4 Lastly, when the relationship is over and you know there will be no reconciliation, it's good to leave that place. Move out of the house or apartment. Move out of state; go and do what you must to get out of that place because staying there is just a constant reminder of what has failed, what has died, the hurt, that pain; staying there is just constantly reminding you that there is no life where you are.

So move on, but as you move on, don't forget to do the same with your mind. Yes, you are moving forward and going to a new place, but you must also move forward in your mind. Change the way you think. Otherwise, you will end up like me, going in circles.

Oh, I almost forgot. There is one thing I didn't tell you. Because I went in circles mentally, I went in circles physically as well. Yep! Even though I moved away to a new place, a new environment, new people, you name it, my life didn't go anywhere because I didn't take my mind with me. But I eventually changed my mindset. I stopped thinking backwards and started thinking forward. But I knew I still had a long way to go.

# CHAPTER 7

## Hello, Sin City

Moving to Las Vegas was a scary move for me, because I had never lived outside of San Diego, California. I didn't know what to expect from Las Vegas nor did I care. At that point in my life, I didn't want to be anywhere after what I had just gone through. But I knew I had to be somewhere stable and peaceful, at least for my kids' sake. So my mother was the answer! She had just purchased a nice big home, where only her and my little brother lived. So that's where I found sanctuary…

Traveling there in a U-Haul truck with a 2-year-old and 4-month-old, you can only imagine what that was like within itself. Not to mention, but I'm going to mention it anyway, I breastfed my 4-month-old. Yes! You heard me right. Terrible, right? So what would usually take me about five hours from San Diego, California to Las Vegas, Nevada, took about nine hours. I had a lot of time to think and try to wrap my mind around what had happened and what was happening. But all I was able to think about was the pain, how heartbroken and angry I was. I mean, what I was feeling at that very moment is unexplainable.

Even though I was on my way to a place of refuge, I still felt helpless, like a failure, and unwanted.

I knew I had to get it together. Pick my life up and figure out what was next for me and my babies.

Once we arrived, it was a relief, because I got there right before night fall. I couldn't imagine being on the road and traveling through those mountains by ourselves. So I was very grateful.

I needed to unpack my things, but I told myself that I would do all of that the next morning. I was way too tired to get it done right away. My mom was so glad that we had made it and that we were now in a safe place.

Days went by, and I didn't leave the house for over a week. The first place I went to was the grocery store with my mother. That was very hard to do because all I wanted to do was ball up in the corner and cry. I wasn't feeling LIFE at that moment. Have you ever gone through something so traumatic that you just didn't care about anything? Including life? Yeah, but I knew I wasn't bold enough to kill myself, nor was I too weak to just give up! So because I was strong and I knew that I wasn't going anywhere, I had a choice to make. I could either lay there and do nothing with myself and let my mom take care of me, or I could actually pick up my life and figure out how I was going to move forward.

So I did just that! I said to myself, "I'm going to be somebody! All these great things I hear about Vegas! People make it here and after what I just went through... Baby, I owe it to myself to be a better person than to lay here in my sorrow and brokenness. So I'm going out! To find and be a better me!"

That motivational speech to myself was awesome! Little did I know, that motivation would lead me right to an ESCORT SERVICE! Yep! Prostitution here I come! And I know what you may be thinking... *"Not The same girl who grew up in church. Not the girl who rededicated her life to God at 18 years old, and surly not the same girl who decided to work out her salvation with fear and trembling."* Yep! That same girl wanted to be a prostitute. Why not!? I figured it wasn't a big deal. There wasn't much to give up being the fact that it was something I was already giving it up for free anyway. So why not make money doing it? It looked like the best thing for me at the time, because again, I had to come up with a solution on how I was going to provide for me and my kids. There was no other way for me... at least that's what I thought.

# CHAPTER 8

## The Call Girl Who Was Never Called

I Googled a couple of agencies and found one that seemed pretty legit, so I gave them a call. A woman answered the phone which immediately made me feel a little comfortable. The phone call was very brief. She asked me a few questions and gave me a day to come down to meet with her, which was a few days after we had spoken.

I was so nervous about the whole thing. Even on the way there, I was just thinking, *what if this is fake, what if they are cops, what if…?* This is something I never did before nor contemplated doing, so I didn't know what to expect.

But I arrived at the place I was told to go. It looked like a rundown office building. I arrived to the suite I was given, knocked on the door, and an older lady answered and greeted me. She took me to a back room where she had a small desk, a computer, and some chairs, and she conducted a smart interview.

She asked me questions like how old I was, what I was willing to do and not willing to do. She took my picture and set up a profile of me on their website. It was definitely something to experience. I was sitting there thinking to myself, *man, this is like a real job interview. Can I get a badge too? Do you give out medical benefits? Retirement?* Of course, I didn't ask those questions, but I sure was thinking it.

After the interview, they gave me instructions and told me to look forward to them calling me. They told me that they would post my picture on their website and if someone liked what they saw then I would get a phone call. I shook the lady's hand and told her thank you before she escorted me out.

I left there feeling so nervous yet so excited because I just knew that I was gonna be bringing in the dough! I got back home and waited for a phone call because I wanted to get to work as soon as possible.

But a couple of days passed by; no phone call. I found it odd because the lady explained to me in the interview that she thought I was beautiful and that my phone would be ringing off the hook. She said that I would have work in no time. So I thought to myself, *well, maybe they probably just need a few more days to warm up. You know, I am new to the website. The men are not used to seeing me on there because I'm new, so they don't know to pick me.*

A few more days go by; still no phone call. I called the agency to find out why I hadn't received a phone call for any jobs.

The lady proceeded to tell me that they don't know why I was not being requested. She said, "You're beautiful. I don't know why our clients are not requesting or at least inquiring about you. I will give you a call once they do. Give it a few more days. I'm sure someone will." I hung up with her and that's exactly what I did.

A week passed by, then before I knew it, three weeks had passed and still no phone call. I decided to call the agency again and they couldn't understand it either. I was desperate and I had to gain income from somewhere because I had to take care of my kids and provide. I could no longer wait on a phone call from them, so I started looking on my own. I was still very nervous about it all and every time I would think about it, I would hear my conscious saying, *you're too good for that, you don't have to do that,* and I would dismiss it. I had to if I wanted to pursue it.

It's so funny because I never considered the reason why I wasn't getting any phone calls.

Later on, I discovered it was because God was protecting me even though it was something I wanted to do. He blocked it and didn't allow it. There is no telling if I had got caught up in that life what would have been waiting for me, either in the beginning or up the road. But now something tells me that I would have never made it that far. Definitely something to be grateful for. Ok, back to the story...

I could no longer wait on the agency to call me. So I went online looking for a man who was looking to have a good time and willing to pay for it. I put myself out there on different popular websites that privately promote prostitution. And moments later, I received my first message.

I was so shocked yet excited and nervous. I couldn't believe it actually worked and someone had contacted me. We messaged back and forth. He told me what he was looking for and what he wanted. I told him that I was available to provide him with a good time. So we set a meet time and he sent me his address. I hurried and

jumped in the shower to get ready. Thank God my kids were out of town with their dads because I didn't have to worry about finding someone to watch them. I hopped in the car, put his address in my GPS, and headed over. It was about 25 minutes from where I lived. Now let me say this, I had the hardest time finding this man's place! It took me about an hour and a half to get to his house because I kept getting lost. Yes, lost! Even though I had the GPS. I thought he gave me the wrong address for a while.

That should have told me right there that I wasn't supposed to go, right? But nope! Your girl was hardheaded. I finally found the right place and parked where he told me to. Now before I got out the car, I prayed. Yes, I prayed. Sounds crazy, right? But isn't that how we do? We get caught up in something we know we don't have any business getting involved in, but ask God to get us out or protect us in it.

Now that I understand how crazy that was, I believe if I was that bold and strong enough to pray before I went in that I could have used that same boldness and prayer to leave.

But you know I went in there! That money was calling my name and I'd come too far to turn back. I hopped out the car and walked up to the door. He was already expecting me so he told me that the door would be left unlocked and to just come in. I slowly opened the door, and while walking in with caution, I said, "Hello?" He replied with "Hi" from the back room. So I stood there in the doorway with the door wide open just in case I needed to make a run for it. Listen, this was my first time doing that and I had to take all precautions.

He came out from the back. I was a little surprised because he was actually handsome. He didn't have much clothing on, just some boxers. He walked over and introduced himself to me. He stood about 5'9. A little on the short side but still taller than me. He was mixed with Indian and Italian, and surprisingly, he was a gentleman. I didn't know why I was surprised by it though. Maybe because of how the movies portray these types of situations. I introduced myself, and after that, he asked me to follow him to the back room.

So I did just that while I looked around for anything that looked suspicious. I followed him into the room, and he closed the door behind me. There was a window, a dresser with the TV on it, and a queen-size bed. The room was nicely put together. He told me that I could have a seat on the bed if I liked.

He walked over to the dresser, opened the dresser drawer, pulled out the money, and handed it to me.

I stood up and started getting undressed. I took all my clothes off and laid on the bed. He took his boxers off and hopped in the bed with me, and we got straight to it. He started kissing me all over my body, starting at the top and made his way down. Come to find out, he had a foot fetish. Good thing I had just got a pedicure the day before. He started to suck on my toes, which I thought was pretty crazy. But hey, the whole thing was crazy so who was I to judge, right?! He then pulled out a condom and he goes to town! The whole time he was on top of me, I'm thinking to myself, *I can't believe you are actually doing this. You did it.* Not really enjoying myself because I was there on a mission, not for pleasure. Even though the sex wasn't bad, my focus was elsewhere. Two hours had gone by and he was finally done. Finally! I thought he would never finish!

I got up and began to put my clothes on, and he starts to tell me how he enjoyed himself and asked my availability to meet again. I told him I would let him know. He put on his boxers, opened the door to the bedroom, and walked me to the front door. We said goodbye to each other. I got in my car and sat there for about 30 minutes, maybe longer. I could not believe what I had just did and that it actually worked, but I could not ignore how it made me feel. Afterwards, I felt dirty, ashamed, disappointed, devalued, you name it. Not to mention, all I could smell was him on my lips and on my body. It wasn't a terrible smell; it was just a smell of someone I didn't know, and that's something I could never get over. I knew once I drove away that I would never go back there again.

When I arrived home, I sat in the driveway and thought about what had just happened. I had decided that prostitution was not for me. I wasn't about that life as they would say. I couldn't shake the way it made me feel. So the very next day, I shut down my accounts and took my pictures and information offline. I couldn't risk anybody messaging me, tempting me to do it again.

I went into the house, and I immediately went to the bathroom and turned the shower on so I could wash all of it down the drain.

I spent about an hour in the shower, maybe a little longer, and once I was done, I hopped out, dried myself off, and started to gather my thoughts and bring myself back together.

Needless to say, I knew prostitution was not for me, and I knew that I still had to figure out how I was going to make money to provide for me and my kids. I put in countless job applications, but I was not receiving any callbacks. I knew I had to figure something out fast because the little child support money wasn't cutting it. A few weeks passed by and still no calls from the job applications I put in. So after days of pondering on what I could do to make some money, I came up with the brilliant idea to possibly try pornography... let the search begin.

# CHAPTER 9

## How Low Can You Go?

I was so shocked to find out how lucrative pornography actually was. I knew that you could make pretty good money doing it, but I didn't know exactly how much I could actually make just by doing one job. This piqued my interest even more, and I just had to have it. My next course of action was to go online to my handy-dandy Google to look up and find listings of people or agencies looking for porn stars. And bingo, I found one. They had an email listed on their ad, so I emailed them right away. The first thing they requested of me was a photo, and of course, a few questions, such as my age, height, weight, location, and so forth. By the time I was done answering all their questions, they wanted to meet with me. I agreed and provided my availability. My meeting with them was in two days during the afternoon. I would have preferred the evening so my mother could watch my kids. Now I had to find someone to watch them.

I didn't have anybody to call really. I was new to Vegas and had lived there for less than a year. I didn't have anyone that I trusted to watch them other than my mother and my brother. I couldn't think of anyone. I said to myself that I would probably have to contact the agency to reschedule. Just as I was getting ready to email them, I remembered an old friend from high school that lived in Vegas. She had been living in Vegas for a few years, and I remembered hooking up with her a few times when I first got out there. She had a child of her own which made me feel a little more comfortable. So I reached out to her, told her I had an interview (well I did), and asked her if it was possible for her to watch my kids while I went to my interview. She didn't hesitate to say yes. I was so thankful to her and very excited. But just like before with the prostitution, I was extremely nervous about it all. I had my doubts about who I spoke with. What if they were a scammer, or a killer for that matter? I wondered if that type of "job" would even work out for me.

So many thoughts ran through my mind. But I could not spend too much time thinking about it. Otherwise, I'd think and talk myself right out of doing it. The day had come, and I got up to get me and my babies ready. I fixed them some breakfast and wash them up; you know, all the common things that you do in the morning. About 30 minutes after that, I headed out the door to drop my babies off at my friend's house. On the way there, I couldn't help not to think about all the "what ifs." You know, all the things that could possibly go wrong. Like what if God decides to kill me in the middle of the act? Or what if I get into a car accident? So many things ran through my mind, and it was because I knew better. But at the moment, I decided not to do better. So I kept on driving. I made it to my friend's house to drop my babies off. She met me outside, so I didn't necessarily have to come in. She helped get them out of the car, and I handed her their bags. I hopped back in the car to head to my meeting. It was a 25-minute drive from where I was. On the way there, I stopped at a gas station just a couple blocks from my destination. I got some gas, breath mints, and water. My mouth was a little dry. I paid for my things, pumped my gas, hopped in my car, and continued toward my destination. My GPS notified me that I had arrived. It was a hotel, one that I will not name. I found parking, grabbed my phone and wallet, and got out the car to head inside the hotel. As I was walking in, I texted the lady I spoke with to inform her that I had arrived. She told me where to go and asked what I was wearing. She wanted to be able to find me easily. I told her that I was wearing a black shirt with light blue ripped jeans. She also told me what color blouse she was wearing so I would be able to spot her out of the crowd as well. I headed to where she told me to stand, which was pretty much in the middle of the hotel. The area was a designated spot for guests to take pictures. I was standing there, nervous as ever, looking for a lady with a red blouse and black bottoms.

While I was looking, a lady comes from behind me and says "Hello, are you, Kellie?" Nervously, I replied yes. I was caught off guard because I wasn't expecting her to find me that fast or to find me first. She shook my hand, introduced herself, and told me to follow her. At that point, I started feeling a little more comfortable but still very nervous. We got in the elevator to head to the room. We go all the way to the top; I believe it was the 24th floor. I started to become a little impressed because I was thinking we must be going to a suite. We got off the elevator and headed down the hall. In about a minute tops, we arrived at the room and she opened the door. I was able to tell that it was definitely NOT a suite, but a very basic room; but what did I expect? These people were conducting porn auditions. But the room was still very nice. There was one guy in the room with a camera. He introduced himself and I did the same. He immediately asked me to get undressed so he could see what I was working with. Well, if I wasn't uncomfortable already, I definitely became uncomfortable then. But I knew it was something I needed to do if I wanted to make the money. Plus, it was what I came for and I couldn't freeze up. So I did exactly what he asked of me and he asked a lot, but I didn't feel too uncomfortable because the lady was still there in the room watching the whole thing.

He asked if I could bend over. He wanted to see how flexible I was so he hog-tied me and stuck his fingers in various places. It was the craziest experience I ever had. Once he was done, he liked what he saw. He then gave me some instructions. He told me to go purchase a dildo, some lubrication, and a medium size butt plug. He said, "Practice with it to loosen yourself up a little bit because you are fairly tight, and if you are trying to be in this industry, you won't last one video." At that point, you can imagine what was going through my head. Not only was I still processing him literally testing my body out with different bondage positions and seeing how many fingers he could place inside me at once, I had to go home and do the same to myself? No sir! I went to the bathroom to wash my hands and myself off a little. They were generous to give me a towel and soap. I put my clothes on and came out the bathroom. I thanked them both; the nice lady that brought me up to the room and the guy that literally did a diagnostic test on my body. I left that hotel room planning to never return again.

Once again, I was not about to do that to my body, nor did I want to go through the mental fight to convince myself to do it. As I was heading to my car, at that very moment, I realized what I had just experienced. I was done with trying to pursue pornography. I hopped in my car and took a deep breath. As I drove away, I started to think about how pornography was not gonna work for me. In a way I was very happy, but on the flipside, I was discouraged because I figured that would be my way out of financial hardship. So there I was back at the drawing board. I still needed to figure out how I was gonna provide for me and my babies. As I was driving to go pick up my kids from my friend's house, I thought to myself, *Well, I have yet to try stripping. You're a great dancer. You can do the splits. You can pop lock. Oh, you got a cute little body that's not completely destroyed by having kids. You just wouldn't be able to take your bra off because your breasts don't sit up where they used to. And you don't want to scare them away, but everything else is good.* I thought about it and planned it all out in my head. Then I snapped out of it! *Who am I kidding? There is no way I'm going to be a stripper. I can't do that. Just as I knew I couldn't do the pornography or prostitution.* I had experienced enough in that world and I say that world because it really is a world of its own that has its own rules; I wanted no part of it. It was short-lived, and overall, I'm glad it was.

It was time for me to do some soul searching. It had dawned on me that I had strayed far away from my upbringing and what I had been taught. I had to get back to what I knew and the only thing I was certain of that did work. And that was church. I did not have a church home, nor did I even think about it. I knew it was time and I couldn't avoid it any longer, neither could I shake the feeling of desiring to be back in fellowship with the people of God. I missed singing and learning about the word of God. So I picked my babies up and thanked my friend for watching them. She asked me how the interview went. I told her it was ok, and that they said they would be in touch with me. She replied, "Good, let me know if you need me to watch them again." I thanked her, gave her a hug, strapped my babies in the car, and headed home. As soon as we got in the house, I got them settled and then began my search for a new church. I Googled churches in North Las Vegas, and so many options came up. I was so excited to get back in a church! And of course, very nervous. I knew that I could Google them, but I had to go visit and experience them if I wanted to make a sound judgment. I came across a church that had an interesting name, which piqued my interest and sounded like the type of church that I was looking for. But little did I know, it wasn't what I expected it to be at all... well, let me just say this... church hurt doesn't exist.

# CHAPTER 10

## Church Hurt and Compromised Sleeping With The Help

This may ruffle a few feathers, but I said it, and I'm not taking it back. Before I even continue, let me just explain what this means.

Church hurt is something very common among the African American Christian community. When someone is a Christian, a member of a church, and experiences hurt by another member/leader of their church or another church, they call it "church hurt."

But is it really? Allow me to give you a different perspective. You may very well indeed experience some type of hurt from another Christian, but it wasn't the CHURCH that hurt you, it was the person that attended church that hurt you. I believe we have to stop making a general statement across the board we're church hurt. When you get hurt by someone at your job, you don't call it job hurt. When your husband or someone hurts you or makes you mad at home, you don't say I'm home hurt, right?

I believe it's just another way to put this black cloud on the church. That way when people hear the word "church", they can associate the name with the pain they felt or are feeling. This can cause the next person who hears about it to reject anything that has to do with the church.

Two things to consider when it comes to these types of things:

1: When one decides to share the hurt that they have experienced in the church, can you please name the church, or if you are the person receiving the information, can you please ask, "What church was it?" That way, the fault doesn't fall on all churches in general.

2: Now, I understand that each offense is different and some things that take place in the church or with people who are Christians could be a unique situation or could not be avoided. I'm not talking about you. I'm speaking to the person who allowed the individual to easily offend you, hurt you, or sleep with you, who used you and then left you high and dry. They did not do it with their own power and might. You had to give them permission. So take full responsibility for your actions and wrongs in the matter, even if your wrong is simply the fact that you allowed them to get to you and under your skin, literally and figuratively. Be honest with yourself and move on. When you do that, I promise you will heal much faster.

3: Just because it's a church, that does not make it a ministry. It's when you start adding members, putting them in the proper position to help with the function and flow of the church, adding auxiliaries, and administering the five-fold ministry is what makes it a ministry. Not the name nor the building.

Just something to consider.

## Sleeping With the Help

How did I get caught up? I had never done anything like this before. I mean, this man was handsome, had so many gifts, and very talented if I may add. He had me, y'all, every part of me. Even the parts I didn't plan to give him. But somehow, he wooed me into being in a place that I couldn't control. Couldn't control my love for him, nor my lady parts when he would come around. His attire was dapper, and he smelled like you just walked into a Macy's. He had me stuck, and I couldn't figure it out for the life of me. The crazy part about it is, I knew it was wrong, but I didn't want to stop feeling for him. He was my drug! And he was also my ELDER.

It all started back when he and I were introduced by a former church member I knew. He and his friend, who was an Apostle, were putting on an event, a youth explosion to be exact. But it turned out to be more like a bomb. If you get where I'm

going. They were looking for a few singers to sing at the event. So she reached out to me, told me about what they had going on, and asked if I would be willing to participate. I told her that I would love to. I wasn't really connected to anybody outside of the church I was attending, so her calling me was a breath of fresh air. She told me that rehearsals would be the upcoming week and would occur a few days out of the week, up until the event. She told me that rehearsal would start at 7 pm at her house. Before we hung up, she offered to pick me up for rehearsal and I gladly accepted her offer.

I was so excited about being a part of the event. I did not know what to expect; I was just happy to be considered. The evening came and she texted me at 6:30 to let me know she was on her way to pick me up. I grab my purse and my water just in case they didn't have any, and I waited close by the door. That way when she pulled up

she didn't have to wait for me to gather my things and run out the door. I believe when someone comes to pick you up, you should not have them waiting for you unless something happens right before, like a wardrobe malfunction or your stomach starts bubbling and you gotta use the bathroom. Other than that, if someone is coming to pick you up, have yourself ready.

Sorry for my rant. Back to my story…

She texted me to let me know she was outside my house. We talked during the drive to her house. It wasn't far; less than a 10-minute drive. On the way there, I was so excited about what it would be like, the songs, and meeting the other singers. We arrived at her home. We get out of the car to head inside, and on the way in, I observed that there weren't any cars outside of her house. So I wondered if anybody was even there yet, or did she pick them up like she did me. We went inside and there were a few people there. She began to introduce me to the few singers that were already there, which was only three people. All women, no men. I didn't find it weird that there were no men, but I guess I was expecting to see a little versatility.

Anyway, I had a seat in the kitchen area because that's where everyone was kinda gathered. The doorbell rung, and one of the ladies ran to answer the door. One of the ladies there said, "That must be them." I wondered who they were talking about. *There are more singers coming?* The young lady opened the door, and in walk two handsome men. One short and the other tall; I'm talking 6'4 tall. I immediately began to focus on the tall one!

He was my type, hunny, from the height to how he carried and conducted himself. Oh yes! I was watching, although I was there to sing. This opportunity had gotten a little more exciting.

Before I got too excited, I started looking for a ring on his finger just to make sure I was not jumping the gun on any others' feelings. I didn't see a wedding ring. I was watching his interaction with the other women, and it was fairly normal. At least from what I could assess. I couldn't say the same for the guy he showed up with though. His interactions weren't normal. He gave off this vibe of being taken, but I didn't see a ring on his finger. As we all know, that doesn't mean anything. Especially nowadays. We did some warmups and he had us go over a few songs, songs that he wrote. Remember I told you he was talented, which made me even more interested. But at the same time, I had to make sure I was focused for the task at hand. I was telling myself, "Cool your panties, Chile." We were there for about two hours. After rehearsal, I found out that the girl that picked me up had to take home another singer she had picked up, and she lived in the total opposite direction from my home. Before I mentioned that I was able to call a ride, HE speaks up and says with so much confidence and assurance, as if he was waiting for the opportunity, "I'll take her home." The girl asked him, "Are you sure?" He replied, "Yes, I'm certain." I had never been more excited to ride home with a stranger in my life. He packed up all the equipment he brought over for rehearsal and headed out to the car. He had a cute lil semi luxury car. He was walking ahead of me and the first thing he did was open the car door for me. At that point it had been a minute since a man had opened a car door for me. So I was loving this already. But I told myself not to get too excited. After all, it was the door to the backseat! That's because the guy he came with was riding with him in the front seat. So what! He still

opened the door for me. So I hopped in. He finished putting everything in the car and we headed out. He told me to direct him to where he needed to go to get me home. And I did just that. It only took us about eight minutes to get to my house. He pulled up to my house and said, "Oh, you live close by. Thank you for tonight, and I'll see you tomorrow for rehearsal." I responded, "Ok, thanks for the ride," before getting out of the car. Nervous to walk away because I knew they were going to be looking, I tried to figure out how hard I was going to switch my hips. As I was walking up the driveway to my door, he rolled his window down and asked, "Hey, will you need a ride for tomorrow?" I said yes, and he said, "Ok, take my number down and text me. That way I can come pick you up." Girrrrllll, this was playing out just like I wanted it to. I ran over to the car so he could give me his number. After he gave me his number,

I thanked him again before saying goodnight. I walked away again, switching a little harder. I went in the house like a schoolgirl who just got asked out on a date by the jock of the school. When I tell you, I danced so hard once I closed the front door. The feeling I had was so fulfilling and packed with excitement of the unknown. Not knowing where this could possibly go. Look at me planning and thinking about the future, and the man just told me to take his number down so he could pick me up for rehearsals. I had already made plans for a future relationship with him in my head. I was silly. And I do mean silly. Little did I know, I would have what I imagined with him and more. I just didn't know it would be something I did not want.

The next day for rehearsal, surprisingly the man kept his promise. Yes, surprisingly, because in that time of my life, I had trust issues. I did not trust anyone. Especially a man after everything I went through.

He showed up every time to pick me up when we were having rehearsal. And that's how we built a little bond and rapport with each other. Soon after that, our conversation went from talking in the car to on the phone. We then found ourselves texting every day. This lasted for about a month. And even after singing at he and his friend's event, we continued talking. I must say the vibe was strong at that point and very evident that he was feeling me, and of course, y'all already know I was feeling him. One evening around 8:30, he texted me and said that he was a little bored at home. He asked if he could come and see me. First off, "a little bored at home"?

I thought to myself, *yeah right*. I texted him back letting him know he could come over. As soon as I put the phone down, I ran to the bathroom. Oh, come on, ladies. Y'all know what that mean. Doesn't mean it's going down, but you must be ready for it just in case, right? He showed up about 20 minutes after he texted me. We headed to the living room where we could chill comfortably. In the living room sat a 75" TV, two nice comfortable couches, and nice lounge decorative chairs that sat next to each other with just a plant arrangement separating them.

So that's where we decided to station ourselves. I grabbed us some bottles of water, and when I tell you we talked for hours! When I finally looked up at the clock, it was 12:30 am, and we were still having good conversation and dialogue with each other. We talked and shared stories about our lives and who we were. It was definitely refreshing. And then he decides to hit me with the words, "I want to kiss you." "You want to kiss me?" I replied to him in my sexy, seductive voice. He said, "Yes, may I?" I leaned toward him and we started kissing. His lips were nice, full, and juicy; juicy meaning non-chapped. We just kept kissing and he pulled back a little, looked me dead in my face, and said, "I want to feel you." I said, "Feel me how?" in my sexy seductive voice. Remember, I had to stay in the mood, so I had to keep talking like that. Ladies, you know, it's what we do so well. He stood up over me and said, "I want to feel you," and started to unbutton his pants. At that point, I was shocked because I imagined a few things with this brotha, but my imagination never went as far as sex. I was thinking along the lines of a possible boyfriend, not just a soul tie.

I looked at him standing over me while he's unbuttoning his pants, and you won't believe what I said to him. I actually shocked myself with my response. I said, "Only if you let me get on top." He sat down so quick! He pulled his pants down to his ankles. I stood up and took my stretch pants off and sat myself right on top of him. And that, my friends, was the beginning of what would eventually come to an end. We went about it for about five minutes, and then I got up. He looked at me like I was a drug and needed another hit. "What are you doing?" he asked. I told him, "You can't get it all tonight. I just wanted to give you a taste." He looked at me with disappointment and said, "Ok, I understand." He pulled his pants up and helped me find mine. I put my pants back on and sat down. I said, "Well, the time has been well spent." It was 1:30 pushing 2 am. I told him that he should probably be heading home. He said, "You're right. I didn't realize how late it actually was." I walked him to the door, and he was kinda holding me from the back while walking. And I was thinking in my head, *could this really be happening to me*? I opened the door and he stood in the doorway. He said, "We'll chat tomorrow? I said yes. He kissed me on the lips and told me to have a good night. After closing the door, I stood there for a while wondering what just happened. Did I really just do that? Did we really just do that? Needless to say, I went to bed a pretty happy woman that night because as far as I was concerned, this was the man of my dreams. He was everything I wanted, plus. I was in La La Land. This man had me.

Over the next few days, we talked over the phone, nothing awkward or weird due to what took place between us. All was good and well. Until one day, he asked me if I could come with him to this church's praise team rehearsal that he played for. I agreed and he told me he would pick me up in a few hours. He arrived to pick me up and it was about a 15 to 20-minute drive with traffic. It was good to see him again, and might I add, he smelled so good! LAWD! I'll tell you, it's something about a good-smelling man. And I'm not talking about Irish Spring or Old Spice. I have nothing against those smells, don't get me wrong. It's just something about a great bottle of cologne. We arrived at the church. It wasn't your traditional-looking church, nor did it have a traditional name. But that was ok. I didn't necessarily judge it by what it looked like, nor where it was located. We walked in and immediately I could tell they must've been a new ministry starting out. I mean, "struggle ministry," but it was a nice snug place, nice chairs, and a cute little pulpit. There was an area for practicing, a keyboard, and a few office spaces, which held the finance office and the pastor's office. When we arrived there, the praise team members were already waiting on him because he played keys for them. It was six of them. This time there were some brothas present. So I was excited. He wanted me to come sing and help out. Everyone introduced themselves to me and there was just one woman out the bunch that stood out to me, but not in a bad way. She had a different aura about her. Everyone else pretty much looked like they belonged. But her? She didn't belong there. I didn't know that woman would become one of my best friends and helpers in life later down the road. We are still very good friends until this day. She was who I gravitated to during rehearsal and any other rehearsals after that. He kept picking me up and taking me with him every week for three weeks straight until finally, I decided I would become a member of the church. Why not? I was there every week helping out and singing with them. So why not just become a member? And of course, what helped my decision was the simple fact that I liked him and had been involved sexually three times at that point. After I joined the next Sunday, that's when things began to shift completely with church as I knew it, and with him and I. Like I said before, the church wasn't traditional looking. It didn't have a traditional name and come to find out, they didn't function the way I knew church to function. It still didn't alarm me because I knew I needed to be in church, and more so I wanted to be with him. So I remained at the church, even in its weird function and state. And him and I? Oh, we were hitting the sheets almost every night for over a year straight. Which I could not understand. I couldn't understand how he and I could be in church faithfully, and not just in church but active members of the ministry and could sleep together knowing it was wrong and continue like nothing was going on between us. I mean,

I was one of the leaders of the praise team and he was a minister, soon to be elder and right-hand man to the pastor. It was bad; we were like rabbits. And I couldn't get enough because he was my drug. It even got to the point where on certain occasions, he would follow me home from a service at church or what have you and we would get it in. I always thought to myself if it would ever become more than what it was with us. Such as us becoming an actual couple. But I eventually realized that it would most likely never happen. Well, couldn't happen, not even if we both wanted to. Because later down the line, I found out that joker was married. He and his wife supposedly were separated. But still very legally married, and by way of a good source still in heavy contact with each other. That not only made me upset, I was a little heartbroken because I not only had high hopes for us, I had fallen in love with this man. Can you believe that? I was in love with a married man, and I never thought I would be in a situation like that. And couldn't figure out how I got to that point for the life of me. I knew that we could no longer be because I feel I had a standard. I'm not one to just go around sleeping with a married man and be aware of it. I felt hurt for his wife and myself. I felt betrayed and used. But sadly, I could not stop sleeping with him. By this time, we had been involved for over a year. And like I told you in the beginning of this chapter, he was my drug. I was addicted him, and what I imagined him to be for me.

My reality was warped because I let this man in and gave him access to parts of me that he should have never been allowed to see, or experience. Nor was he worthy to. I knew I had to do something to stop this entanglement. And I had to do it fast because I kept feeling bad every time we would have sex. Isn't that funny though? I would feel bad about what I was doing because I found out about his wife, but didn't feel bad knowing God wasn't pleased with my actions. Says a lot about the church I was going to as well, because I knew a few of the praise team members had picked up on us by then. And I'm almost certain the pastor knew but never said a word to me. But I don't blame the pastor. I used to though. Because how can I sit up in your church as a member and not just that, but by then as the pastor's assistant, and you never say anything to me about sleeping with your right-hand man. But I made those choices, not her. But allow me to give you a little tip.

If you are a member of a church, and you observe someone commit sin, or you yourself are able to commit sin and different acts freely, take a closer look to the leader and operations of the ministry. Because there is no way you should be able to attend/be part of a church and still do all your dirt, no conviction about it from Sunday to Sunday and not be led or called out to correct it. Whether by way of your pastor calling you out personally or during the message, or by conviction. Just something I have learned over the years.

So needless to say, I found my conviction and my worth. I decided to just cut him off, cold turkey. I knew I had to because for me, there was no winging off him. I either had to do it and be done with him or be stuck forever and risk popping up with the package. Then I would really be stuck with something I didn't want. Which would be him or the baby. I'd be lying if I said it wasn't hard for me. Day after day, I thought about going back, but I knew I couldn't do that. I had already closed that door. Which leads me to my second tip.

If you have closed the door on an entanglement, that door should remain closed. Do not sit there staring at the door, entertaining the thought of opening it back up. Close it, lock it, toss the key, walk away, and never return to it again. I'm sorry to be the one to tell you, but it's not going to just magically change. No, you can't stay while they work through their issues. No, you can't change them. They have to desire to change on their own. And no, God did not call them to be your spouse. RUN and never look back.

**Because that is exactly what I did. I ran, and I never looked back.**

# CHAPTER 11

## Finding My Worth and My Happily Ever After

He stood about 6'3 230 pounds (nice and muscular like I like them), with light to medium brown skin, nice feet and hands. Clean cut, a beautiful smile, and he smelled so amazing! Yes, that was the description of my dream man! And what I wrote down on my list. The list that my sister in Christ from church had me do. I forgot to tell you, I joined a new church! And once I joined, I gained a new family. It has all types of outreach programs, and different auxiliaries that you can be a part of, depending on what you need or are seeking.

She was over the marriage ministry, and during that time, she had been married for nine years. And she is an activist for "dating God's way," so you can have the proper love and possibly marriage that God wants and desires for you to have. So anyone that was thinking about dating or was already dating, she was the one you wanted to talk to, honey.

She had me write what I desired when it came to dating someone. Of course, I started with his looks. I mean, I know his character and the qualities that he possesses are what's important, but on the flip side of that, the negro has to be attractive, right?.. anyway!

Once I finished my list, I handed it over to her. She had me and my cousin sitting at her dining room table filling out this "list," and I'm not going to lie, it was very clever, and more importantly effective on how she had us do it. I reached across the table to hand it to her and she took mine. She then looked at my cousin to ask her if she was done with her list. My cousin looked stressed out, and she replied as if she was scared and nervous. We began to laugh so hard. She finally finished hers, and then my sister in Christ looked at them both and handed them back to us. That's when she began to ask us both questions. Questions on what really mattered; are certain things on our list necessary, what are some deal breakers, what are you willing to compromise on, and a whole lot of other questions that really had me thinking.

After she was done asking me all the questions she had, I started to see how shallow I was. How the things on my list were what I had always desired and aimed for in a man. The men I was attracted to and or serious about, they all had that same similar look and build. And it had gotten me nowhere but hurt, broken, disappointed, and possibly with the package, which is a baby.

I realized for the very first time in my life that I had to do something totally different than what I had done in the past. And that was trust God concerning dating and a possible husband, which is something I had never done.

As I sat there at her dining table, I came to some realities that I had yet to have a successful relationship, which was why I was single and a double baby momma. And I was tired of that! I knew deep down inside there was more for me. And I knew that I deserved to be loved the right way.

So I got up out of my chair, tore the list up, and went to throw it in the trash can. I came back to the dining table where they both watched what I had just did. I said to them both that I was done with that list. I was

done with the things that I desired. I was done with the things I thought I wanted. It was clear that I didn't know what I needed in a boyfriend or spouse. I decided that I was just going to totally commit myself to God, and if I did that, I believed he would send the right man my way. And I never looked back. I never went back on what I said. I never tried to create another list, and to be honest, I never thought about it again after that day. I was truly done with how I was doing things as it pertained to men.

And because I submitted myself to God and told him that I trusted him, trusted him to give me exactly what he knew I needed and desired in a man, I saw quick results! I like to call it my New Beginning.

During one Sunday morning, about three weeks after the "list" session, we were all at church. I was ushering that day, standing at the front door, greeting the people with a smile as they came in. Church was starting soon, and people were rolling in being seated. In comes my sister in Christ and her husband flying up to the church because they were running a little behind. They parked and hopped out of the car, and surprisingly, they brought a visitor with them who got out of the backseat of their car. I had a bird's eye view! She didn't tell me that they were bringing a visitor to church with them. Let alone a man. I mean she didn't have to inform me of that, but we're pretty close so I thought maybe she would have mentioned it. Well, anyhow, they started walking up to the door to come inside and I was trying to get a good look at this brotha!

They all walked in and I'm one of the first people they see. She introduced him to the people standing ahead of me. And then it was my turn to be introduced. She said, "Hey Kellie, this is my brother in-law who just moved here and now staying with my husband and I. Brother, this is Kellie." I said, "Nice to meet you. Welcome." He said thank you and kept walking to find a seat. That was it. Nothing more, nothing less. And that being because once I got a good look at him, he wasn't "my type" per se. He was short, stood about 5'9, dark-skinned, had glasses, and on another note, he had a perm. And if it wasn't a perm, he had some thick waves on his head. Listen, I'm all for something different, but a man with a perm is a deal-breaker for me.

After that, I never thought about it or him.

Until one day, shortly after the day we met, he showed up to church looking different. To me, it looked like he had gotten a makeover or something of that sort. He went up to the altar to get prayed for and that is when things shifted for me. I saw him for the first time in a light of being attractive. I had never looked at him as such when I would see him from Sunday to Sunday. But for some reason, this Sunday was different. I even remember what he had on. Raspberry purple dress shirt, black slacks, caramel brown belt with caramel brown shoes, to be exact! And his hair was cut neatly with waves. And his wave game was on point if I may add. He didn't have the struggle waves. From that day forward, anytime I would see him at church, I could not take my eyes off him. My attraction became stronger and stronger, and I couldn't understand it. I would talk and confide in a couple of church members I was close to at the time, telling them how I felt, and how weird it was for me. Because I had never even thought twice about being with this guy, and what felt like overnight, I was attracted to him and couldn't stop thinking about him as if he put a spell on me. I felt like I had literally been shot by Cupid!

A week passed, and I had dreamed about him, daydreams of him hugging me and kissing me! So you can imagine at that point I was so confused. I didn't know how it happened and I needed to do something about it. Because if I didn't, I was going to go crazy!

It was another Sunday and we were in church as usual. And just like any other Sunday, I not only couldn't stop looking at him, I couldn't stop thinking about him. I was always cute, but I made sure I was extra cute that day so he would notice me when I walked around during offering. Yes, I was a mess.

After church, I said to myself that I needed to say something to him besides "hi" and "how are you doing?" But I didn't know what to say nor how to lead into what I really wanted him to know. A sista felt like I was in grade school all over again. Maybe I should just write him a note with three boxes on it that says "check one…will you be my boyfriend?

Yes, no, or maybe…"

But I couldn't do that because that would be me chasing him. But I knew better because what the word of God says:

*"Whoso findeth a wife findeth a good thing, and obtaineth favour of the Lord"* (Proverbs 18:22).

Plus, my pastor was big on that because we had a lot of single women in our church and he would always remind us to allow the man to do the shopping. "Don't be out there jumping in baskets." I said, "Ok Kellie, you can't approach him because that would be too obvious, especially because you don't even say more than a few words every time you see him." I had to be clever and quick because there was no way I could go another day feeling this way without saying something to him.

So I left church. And I was one of many to leave last because we had to stay to clean up the sanctuary. But I could not wait to get home because while cleaning the church, I came up with an idea on how I was going to try to spark a conversation with him. And that was to inbox him on social media. I forgot that I had him as a friend there. I was excited. I drove home nervous and anxious! Wait, why am I always driving home anxious and nervous? That seemed to be my thing over the years. That is too funny.

Well, I got home, ran in the house, changed, showered, and settled myself. I sat on my bed and stared at my phone, wondering what I was going to say to this man.

I just went with my first mind. What did I have to lose, right? Here goes nothing!

I opened up my messages on social media, found his name, and clicked on it to message him. I typed,

"Hey, I just want you to know that you looked really nice today! I liked the color of your shirt." I mean, what else was I going to say? I didn't want to be general because that was how all of our interactions had been in the past. So I didn't want that type of dialogue because if you know like I know, it's hard to move on in the conversation when it starts off general, especially when you really want to talk about the real stuff.

I pressed send scared as all get out! Because I didn't know what this man's response would be. Or if he would respond at all! About 30 minutes go by and I started to lose it because I hadn't gotten a response back. What if he thinks my message was lame and not respond? And then I'll be left looking stupid! Ugh! I walked away from my phone for another 30 minutes or so because it was torture waiting for a response.

I came back to my phone to see that he had finally replied to me! With surprise, excitement, and nervousness, I opened the message and it said these words: "Oh, thanks. That is very nice of you. You looked very beautiful today yourself." My eyes bulged out of my head and I practically melted! I was so excited and relieved that he responded, and over the moon that he replied with a compliment to me. And not just a general compliment. He stated that I looked "Very Beautiful." I screamed like a school girl, and before I could reply to him with a "thank you," he followed up with another message, making conversation with me. We talked endlessly that night. And for hours the days after that, all throughout the whole week. There wasn't a day we didn't speak. It had gotten to where we would fall asleep on the phone with each other. Our chemistry, our connection, was perfect. He was so sweet, and such a gentleman. I was really feeling this man! And it was clear he was feeling me because just three weeks after our initial conversation, he asked me to be his girlfriend. And of course, I said yes!

Just six months after that, he surprised me with an amazing engagement that involved over 30 people made up of family and friends, and that does not include the people that were there to watch.

Then seven months after that, we had a beautiful wedding and reception with over 165 guests in attendance. And lastly, eight months after our wedding, I found out that I was pregnant with our first baby girl on Father's Day. We named her Promise.

I was in awe of what God had done and how fast he did it! All because I decided to chuck that list two years prior. I allowed him to send me the man that he knew I needed and that I didn't know I wanted. And when I tell you, this man is everything I need and wanted! He's all that plus some! God knew exactly what He was doing. And He definitely showed out on my behalf.

I'd like to encourage you. If you are a woman looking for a husband, my first tip will be to stop looking, and start looking for God and what he desires. Now, I know it's easier said than done, trust me! It clearly took me years to figure it out, and when I failed, I couldn't figure it out for the life of me! I didn't know what I was doing wrong, but you either want to keep missing it because you can't subject yourself to him, or you can let go of all that you think you may know and want and allow him to send you what you're supposed to have.

Trust me, you'll be glad that you did. Plus, it'll be so worth it in the end. Because then you'll also have the testimony of living your "Happily Ever After." I'm finally happy after everything I have been through. Now I no longer have to go through life saying, "I can't figure this out for the life of me." This is the true life of me, because I have allowed God to do it.

Thank you for reading.

## Connect with me on Facebook and Instagram

CPSIA information can be obtained
at www.ICGtesting.com
Printed in the USA
LVHW051001200422
716608LV00008B/944